THE CHESTNUT PAN

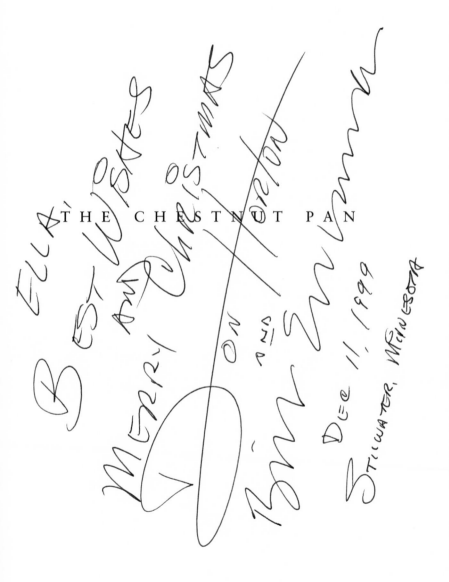

ELLA,

Best Wishes
and Merry Christmas
on Don Horton
and

Bill Emmer

Dec 11, 1999
Stillwater, Minnesota

THE
CHESTNUT
PAN

A CHRISTMAS STORY

Written by Donald Horton

Illustrated by William Ersland

PUMPKIN BREAD PRESS
Saint Paul, Minnesota

ISBN 0-9663750-0-9

FIRST EDITION
02 01 00 99 98   7 6 5 4 3 2 1

Printed in the United States of America

Pumpkin Bread Press
2015 Dayton Avenue
St. Paul, Minnesota 55104

For my family

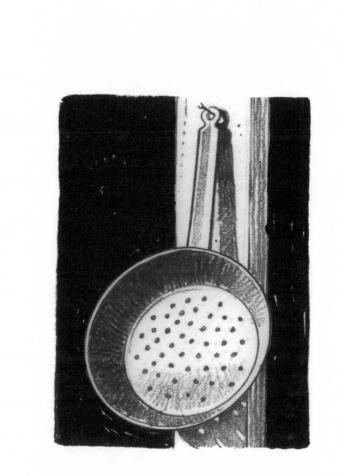

*I*N FRANKLIN TOWNSHIP the snow fell softly, covering the Olson farm and the fields beyond. It was Christmas Eve. Jon Olson sat cross-legged before the glowing fire he'd built, and in his lap rested a chestnut pan. Its weight and familiarity offered some comfort against the sadness that hung over him on this night. He wondered, as he often had lately, if this was the last Christmas the Olson family would spend together at the farmhouse.

"Daddy, what are you thinking about?" Jon's daughter, Kari, who had just turned nine, interrupted his thoughts. She was sitting beside her great-grandmother's rocking chair, which had stood empty since that fall when Nora Olson, Jon's grandmother, died.

Jon didn't answer right away. He looked up at the mantel where a worn statue of St. Patrick stared solemnly ahead. Jon smiled. He knew it was unusual for a Lutheran family to display a Catholic saint at Christmastime, but it was a cherished family tradition.

"With both my grandma and grandpa gone, Kari, Christmas Eve doesn't seem quite the same," he said.

From the kitchen they could hear the voices of Kari's mother and the many relatives who had gathered at the farmhouse for dinner. But here by the fire all was quiet, except for the occasional snap as the logs shifted.

"I just don't know how long we'll keep getting together at the farm like this," Jon continued.

He pulled a handful of chestnuts from a brown paper bag beside him and placed them in the chestnut pan. Then he took his jackknife from his pocket, opened the large blade, and carefully began to slit each nut crosswise on the rounded side, just as his grandfather, Carl Olson, had done every Christmas Eve in years past.

"But Daddy, we're still a family. And we'll always have the farm. Won't we?"

"We've agreed to keep it for now. But things change."

"What if we don't want them to?" she asked.

Jon looked at his daughter and gave her a reassuring hug. "Things always change, honey."

Kari watched as he arranged the chestnuts flat side down in a tightly packed single layer in the pan, which he placed into the fire. Flames licked the sides as it balanced on the logs; the heat turned the pan's color from silver to smoky black.

"Christmas is a time of new beginnings," said Jon. "Those were your great-grandmother's words."

Kari could see the sadness in her father's eyes. She reached for a small stack of papers near the Christmas tree. "Read me the story, Daddy," she said, snuggling up to him. "The one you wrote about Great-Grandma and Great-Grandpa, and the chestnut pan."

"Okay," he answered. "But first, hand me a piece of kindling. I need to stir the chestnuts so they don't burn."

"Don't burn the chestnuts, or we won't let you roast them next year," said Kari.

Jon looked at her, and they both laughed, knowing Nora had said those very words to Carl the first time they roasted chestnuts together. Carl had pretended to be offended and said rather matter-of-factly that he knew how to roast chestnuts; of course, he proceeded to burn the first batch. After that, every year Nora would tease Carl with the familiar warning and Carl would chuckle in reply. The words became a stitch weaving each Christmas into the tapestry of Christmases gone by.

Jon held the papers in his hand. For a moment, he looked into the hearth, and the shadows of the flames dancing on the back wall gave way to a picture of the farm when he was a little boy. As he began to read, he could hear his grandparents' voices once more.

THE
OLSON'S IRISH
CHRISTMAS

by Jon Olson

Presented to the
Franklin Township
Historical Society

In Loving Memory of
Carl and Nora Olson

ARL AND NORA OLSON lived their entire lives in Franklin Township. They were childhood sweethearts. Everyone in town expected them to marry, and they did. Not everyone remembered the date, but they all remembered the year. It was the spring of 1931, during the Great Depression, the same year the Mississippi flooded all of Franklin Township up to Griswold's farm.

Just about everyone in the small Lutheran township was Norwegian—born and raised on a farm—and Carl and Nora were no exception. The story went that Reverend Finn Jenson chose a site for building his church—Divine Redeemer Lutheran—on a large ridge overlooking the Mississippi to the east and the Zumbro river to the south. The church became a beacon to the hundreds of hard-working and upright Lutheran immigrants looking for a place to put down roots. When Franklin Township was founded, it was the only all-Lutheran township in Minnesota.

In the summer of 1931, Carl and Nora inherited a small plot of land with an old clapboard farmhouse and a barn. Carl had saved some money so they could afford to buy a few chickens and two cows. It was generally agreed in the town that all signs pointed to a good life together for the young couple.

Work on the farm kept Carl and Nora busy that first summer. They rose at dawn each day, and while Carl milked the cows, Nora prepared a hearty breakfast. After breakfast, Carl would head to the fields to tend the rich earth. Nora fed the chickens, gathered eggs, and weeded her garden. By autumn, Carl and Nora were expecting their first child.

"Carl," Nora said one night. "These chilly feet of mine mean for sure it's a baby boy."

"I'll build a fire for you, dear," Carl answered. He knelt by the hearth to light the kindling.

"You're so good to me, I want to name the baby after you," Nora told him.

"Let's hope it's a boy then," Carl replied.

One thing was certain: The entire township expected another good Norwegian name to be added to the congregation of Divine Redeemer Lutheran the following spring.

❄

The week before Thanksgiving, Nora was in the basement stocking the shelves with fruits and vegetables she had canned from her garden. It was then she first noticed the odd-looking pan hanging on a beam in the far corner.

The pan had deep sides and a pattern of holes on the bottom. "What could you possibly cook in a pan with holes in it?" she wondered aloud. She placed it in a burlap seed bag and brought it to the church potluck dinner that night to ask some of the other women what the pan was used for.

Someone said, "That's a chestnut pan, Nora. For roasting chestnuts over a fire."

Someone else added, "Italian chestnuts are best."

The idea of roasting chestnuts with her new husband sounded cozy and romantic to Nora. Although she had never roasted chestnuts herself, she remembered childhood stories of people who had. "We can roast chestnuts every Christmas," she thought. "It will be our first family tradition."

Before bed that night, she told Carl that all she wished for this Christmas was a bag of chestnuts, preferably the Italian kind.

❋

On December 23, Carl went to nearby New Oslo to do his Christmas shopping. The cradle he'd made to surprise Nora was hidden in the barn, and all he had left to do was to purchase his wife's special gift. He parked his pickup truck in front of Nelson's General Mercantile on Main and walked in to buy one pound of Italian chestnuts.

"Good morning, Hans," said Carl as he entered the small store.

"Morning, Carl." Hans Nelson stood behind the counter. The store was filled with Christmas smells—cinnamon, evergreen, and special goods Nelson's carried this time of year.

"Nora asked for chestnuts for Christmas. Need about a pound."

"Don't carry chestnuts, Carl. Except by special order."

"But you carry peanuts, don't you?"

"Yep."

"And walnuts?"

"Yep. But I don't carry chestnuts, except by special order. Too expensive."

"Where can I get some then?"

"Closest place is St. Paul. O'Hara's General Store should have them—O'Hara carries most everything. He's a big Irish Catholic fella. I hear it's best you don't let him know you're a Lutheran, though, or he won't sell you anything."

"O'Hara's, you say?"

"Yep, on the levee. Can't miss it."

Carl left the store and knew he had a problem. St. Paul was a three-hour drive when the weather was good. The skies had been a steely gray for days, and like most farmers, Carl could sense a snowstorm coming—most likely a big December blizzard that would have the town digging out for days. He had too much work around the farm and couldn't spare a full day chasing after a bag of chestnuts. It just wasn't practical, and if a good Norwegian farmer in Franklin Township was anything, he was practical.

As Carl drove home, he thought about his new wife and her Christmas wish. Nora never asked for much, and it was just like her to want a small gift that would mean a lot. He couldn't remember a day when he hadn't loved her, and he didn't want to disappoint her on their first Christmas morning as husband and wife.

Carl went into the house, removed his heavy boots, and shook off the cold. He found Nora in the kitchen, standing at the sink washing the chestnut pan. She gazed out the kitchen window and said, "I was getting worried about you. I think there's a storm on the way, and it looks like a bad one."

Carl stood there in silence. He wondered how to explain to his wife that he needed to go to St. Paul in the morning.

"Carl, I'm talking to you. Are you all right?" Nora wiped her hands and turned to face him.

He thought about all the work he had to do and how impractical a trip to the city was at this time of year. He started to form the

words, "I couldn't get the chestnuts you wanted." What came out was, "I have to go to St. Paul tomorrow."

"St. Paul? For heaven's sake, what for?"

"Uh, things," he stammered.

"Things? What things? Tomorrow's Christmas Eve."

"Just things," Carl said more boldly. "It's important, and I can't talk about it."

Nora pressed him for an explanation, but the more she questioned him, the more closed-mouthed he became. She was confused and hurt, and she wondered if the trip to St. Paul had something to do with the farm. Were they in financial trouble? Olson men, true to their Norwegian heritage, weren't known for sharing their feelings, but it was unlike Carl to shut her out completely. By the time they went to bed, Carl and Nora weren't speaking, and for the first time in their marriage they didn't kiss goodnight.

Early the next morning, Carl rushed through his chores. He noticed the wind was colder and from the east. Thick clouds, heavy with snow, hung low over the farm. For a moment, he considered staying home.

"No, I can beat the storm," he thought.

When he went in for breakfast, the kitchen table was bare except for a brown paper bag. A note pinned on its corner read "Have a nice time in St. Paul." Carl opened the bag and pulled out an egg salad sandwich wrapped in waxed paper. He hated egg salad. He knew he was in trouble, but he wasn't about to tell Nora the real reason he was going to the city.

The truck started right away despite the cold, and Carl thought it was a good sign. But just north of New Oslo, the snow began to fall. Carl got on the county road heading west. No one else was on the road.

Bare trees darkened the rolling hills of the Zumbro river valley. Carl remembered how he had always thought trees in winter looked plain until Nora said how much she liked them. She called them the "lacy trees of winter" because of the intricate patterns the leafless branches made against the sky.

Layers of snow covered the hills and fields. All along the county road, the barns were shut tight to the rising wind. In the gray stillness, Carl could see little rectangles of pale light—the windows of the farmhouses—with people preparing for the holiday, safe and warm inside. He wished he were home.

He had almost reached the highway when he saw the cemetery, and he knew he had entered Lake Florence Township. With its wrought iron fence in front and barbed wire around the sides and back, the cemetery had always made Carl uneasy. There were two entrances: The east side had the words "St. Mary's Catholic Cemetery" spelled out in small wrought iron letters, but the west entrance read "Emmanuel Lutheran Cemetery." Unless you were from Lake Florence Township and knew the people buried there, you couldn't tell where the Lutherans ended and the Catholics began.

On the pillars beside the cemetery gates, stone angels appeared to hover in the blowing snow. Carl felt as if they were watching him as he drove by. He was thankful that when his time came, he'd be buried in Divine Redeemer Lutheran Cemetery, which had only one entrance and no angels.

He reached Highway 61 and drove north toward the city. Even on a gray and snowy day like today, the landscape had a quiet beauty. As the snow drifted and swirled in the light of the headlamps, Carl shivered beneath his winter coat. It was cold in the truck, and he had a long way to go.

✻

The snow nearly doubled the time it took Carl to get to St. Paul. By late afternoon he had reached the levee, and all around him the streets and storefronts were quiet. He found O'Hara's and parked the truck.

Carl went to the front door and turned the handle, only to find it locked. In his anticipation, he hadn't noticed the sign that read "Closed until Dec. 26. Have a Merry Christmas." His stomach sank. It had never occurred to him that the store would be closed. "Of course it's closed," he thought. "Nelson's isn't open on Christmas Eve, either."

Carl brushed away frost and snow and peered through the window, hoping to catch a glimpse of someone inside. He saw shelves lined with cans, flour, sugar, and coffee. Barrels and boxes of goods stood against the far wall. Then he spotted something that made him catch his breath. Above a barrel in the corner was a small sign: "Italian Chestnuts, 12 cents a pound."

He pounded on the door and yelled, "Hello! Is anybody in there?"

Silence.

He pounded again, harder this time. "Is anyone there?"

A sharp voice cut the cold air. "Stop your racket, we're closed!" The voice came from the direction of heaven, but it definitely was not a heavenly voice. Carl stepped back and looked up. A large bald head stuck out of a second story window.

"Mister, do you run this store?"

"Run it? I own it," snapped the man. "I'm Sean O'Hara and like the sign says, we're closed."

"I can see the sign, sir, but I need some chestnuts," Carl said to the Irishman.

"Then you should have been here when we were open."

In the wintry air, with the cold piercing his skin, Carl was beginning to feel a little desperate. "I've been on the road since morning. The snow slowed me," he said. "I drove up from Franklin Town——" Carl cut short his words. Hans had warned him not to mention he was Lutheran, and by saying he was from Franklin Township, Carl had done just that.

O'Hara looked down with a scowl. "I'll bet your name is Sorenson and you're a Lutheran," said O'Hara.

"My name is Carl Olson, and I am a Lutheran, sir. Everyone in Franklin Township is."

"I know, which is why it gives me great pleasure to tell you not to bother coming back at all," said O'Hara, spitting out the words.

At that moment, a woman appeared next to O'Hara, her red hair giving away her Irish heritage. "What's going on, dear?"

"A Norwegian Lutheran from Franklin Township is here for some chestnuts and doesn't seem to understand that decent stores close to honor the holiday. So I'm sending him packing," replied O'Hara. He began to close the window.

"Wait!" Carl shouted. "At least listen to me."

Mrs. O'Hara stopped the window with her hand. "We'll listen."

O'Hara folded his arms. Carl could see the man was annoyed.

"I admit it to you and yours, sir. I am a Norwegian Lutheran from Franklin Township. But this past spring I got married, and now my wife is expecting. This fall she found an old pan in our basement, and she says it's for roasting chestnuts. All she wants for Christmas is Italian chestnuts for roasting in her pan."

Carl waited for a response, and when he heard nothing, he continued to talk—not even sure the O'Haras were listening. He pulled off his hat and held it to his chest. "I told her I would get her some chestnuts, thinking I could buy them in town. But the man who runs the general store told me O'Hara's was the only place that sold them these days."

Again Carl waited for a reply, but there was only silence from the open window.

He tried to think of something more he could say to convince the O'Haras to open the shop. He decided if the truth wouldn't persuade them, perhaps a lie would.

"I know you're Catholic. We've always spoken highly of Catholics in our home," he said. He stood in the wind, waiting for an answer. The snow flew around him and landed in cold spatters on his bare head.

"I know you don't like Lutherans," he continued, "but it seems to me that when we celebrate Christmas, we celebrate the birth of the same baby Jesus, don't we?

"It's my first Christmas with my wife, and I don't want to let her down. Please don't send me away empty-handed."

Carl realized begging made him feel very alone and very cold. He thought Joseph must have felt like this while looking for a room for Mary that night in Bethlehem.

Mrs. O'Hara said, "Sean, that boy may be Norwegian, but with blarney like that I think we could make him an honorary Irishman for one day, don't you?"

"And what next, make him an honorary Catholic? Go on with you now. Next you'll tell me he'll be praying to the Blessed Virgin tonight," O'Hara answered coldly.

Mrs. O'Hara touched her husband's shoulder. "Look at him, Sean. He's no more than a boy. He's not only talking Irish, he's acting Irish. What he's doing for his wife any self-respecting Irishman would do for his. And I know that what this boy's doing Sean O'Hara would do for his own wife."

Carl saw O'Hara look at his wife and then shake his head. "All right, all right," he said. "Boy, put your hat back on and go around to the back door. I'll let you in."

"Yes, sir!"

Carl hurried to the back of the store, wading through rising drifts of snow. In the darkness of the alley, he heard a door slam shut above him. Heavy footsteps pounded on the stairs, growing louder with each step. Hans Nelson had said O'Hara was a large man, and Carl was starting to get nervous. Why had O'Hara made him come to the back door? Was it because he didn't want anyone to see him go in?

Carl suddenly realized that if no one saw him go in, no one would know if he never came back out.

The snap of a deadbolt jolted him back to reality. The back door swung open.

"Get inside," ordered O'Hara.

Carl looked up at the huge bulk of a man and stood there, unsure whether to obey.

"I said get in."

Carl gingerly stepped over the threshold, and the door shut behind him with a thud. He watched O'Hara turn the deadbolt, then swiftly pick up full fifty-pound kegs of nails in each hand as if they were empty.

"Follow me," said O'Hara gruffly. Carl followed him along a dark, narrow pathway that led through a crowded storeroom. The wooden floor creaked beneath the weight of their footsteps.

As they walked toward the front of the store, O'Hara said, "I'm keeping the lights off. Don't want anyone to know you're in here."

Carl nodded as if he understood, even though he didn't understand and wasn't sure he wanted to. He smelled coffee beans and thought of Hans Nelson's store back home. Other unfamiliar scents—Cuban cigars, foreign spices, and Florida oranges in crates— filled the store. He followed a few steps behind O'Hara with his nose in the air, sniffing like a hunting dog.

O'Hara spun around and faced him. "You got a cold, boy?" he demanded.

Carl jumped back, startled, and his arm hit a vegetable bin. "No, sir," he said. A squash toppled from the bin, fell to the floor, and split open. Carl stared at O'Hara, who was angrily looking at the mess.

"Pick that up," said O'Hara.

"Yes, sir," said Carl, picking up the broken squash and resting it on the bin.

"Quit your sniffing and watch where you're going."

"Yes, sir," Carl replied sheepishly.

O'Hara put the kegs of nails against the far wall and pointed to the chestnut barrel. "There," he said. "Help yourself. And hurry up."

Carl walked over to the barrel thinking, "If he tries anything, I can make a run for the front door. I can throw vegetables at him to slow him down." He glanced over his shoulder at O'Hara, who was watching his every move. With his hands shaking slightly, Carl picked up the scoop and filled a small tin pail with chestnuts.

O'Hara went behind the counter and waited, and Carl carried the pail to him. "Here," he said, sliding it across the counter. "That's all I'll need."

O'Hara poured the chestnuts into a paper bag and handed them back to Carl, all the while looking out the front window facing the levee. Carl realized O'Hara was worried someone might see them inside and start asking questions—that's why he was keeping the lights off. If word got out that Sean O'Hara had opened his store on Christmas Eve for a Lutheran from Franklin Township, his business in the Catholic neighborhood might be ruined.

"Don't you want to weigh the chest-nuts?" Carl asked.

"I know how much you got," O'Hara replied. "The only reason you're getting these at all is because you charmed Mrs. O'Hara."

Carl nodded. He would pay whatever O'Hara asked; he was in no position to bargain.

Then Carl noticed a row of St. Patrick statues for sale behind the counter. Each one had painted green eyes, except for a statue on the first shelf, which had blue ones. As Carl studied the mysterious blue-eyed statue, a feeling of calm came over him. He felt like he was going to be all right, and the more he gazed into the eyes of the statue, the safer he felt. He thought that perhaps he might even come back to the store again sometime.

O'Hara seemed to read his mind. "Don't think you can come back here ever again," he snapped. "I only let you in to keep peace at home."

Carl handed O'Hara the 12 cents he owed him. "One more thing," he said.

"What is it?" asked O'Hara impatiently.

"I lied to you when I said Catholics were always spoken well of in our home."

"Well now, what a surprise," replied O'Hara, placing his hands on his hips, his voice heavy with sarcasm.

"But, sir, in the future it will be different. I want to purchase one of your St. Patrick statues. I promise that every Christmas Eve when we roast chestnuts, we'll say a prayer of thanksgiving to him for your kindness."

O'Hara let out a laugh. "Deliver me from that kind of talk. A Norwegian's prayers to the Saint of Ireland won't do any good."

O'Hara reached for a statue from the shelf.

"Not that one," said Carl. "The one with the blue eyes, please."

"It should have green eyes. St. Patrick had green eyes. That one's a painting mistake," said O'Hara.

"I'd like it anyway," replied Carl.

"Protestants," said the Irishman, shaking his head.

O'Hara balanced the blue-eyed statue in the bag with the chestnuts. "No charge. It will be payment enough to know that a Lutheran in Franklin Township is praying to St. Patrick once a year."

They walked back down the hall.

"Merry Christmas to you, sir, and to Mrs. O'Hara," Carl said, stepping through the back door.

O'Hara stuck his head out and looked up at the snow, which was still falling fast. "Listen, boy," he said. "That's a mean storm. This isn't a safe night for any man, Catholic or Lutheran, to be out on the road. Be careful . . . and Merry Christmas."

Carl nodded, and O'Hara nodded back and closed the door.

As Carl drove home, the snow finally stopped but the wind shifted from the north, blowing the fallen snow so fiercely that it appeared to be snowing sideways. He could barely see the road. The wind soon picked up speed over the rolling fields, piling the snow into knee-deep drifts across the highway. Every so often, Carl could feel the truck sliding toward the shoulder, and he would wrestle the steering wheel to stay on the road.

Just before Carl reached the county road, a strong gust tossed a blanket of snow over the windshield. He took his foot off the gas pedal and tried to hold the steering wheel steady as the truck slowed. Suddenly the truck swerved and lurched downward. He gripped the wheel tightly and shut his eyes. The truck swung upward and hit something that didn't give way, bringing the vehicle to an abrupt halt. Carl's head hit the back window with a thump.

❄

By eight o'clock that evening, Nora was sick with worry. She began to call the neighbors to find out if anyone had heard from Carl. One of her calls reached Hans Nelson. When she told him Carl had gone to St. Paul but wouldn't tell her why, Hans said he was certain it was to buy chestnuts.

"Chestnuts?" Nora couldn't believe her ears. "Why would he have to go all that way?"

"Like I told Carl, I don't carry chestnuts anymore. Only place I know of that does is O'Hara's on the levee."

"I made him eat egg salad," she replied.

"What's that you say?"

"Nothing," she said. "If you hear from Carl, please call me right away."

Nora put another log on the fire just to have something to do. She remembered that Carl had left thinking she was angry with him; she was, of course, but she didn't want him to die in a blizzard with that as his last memory of her. She went into the kitchen to get the chestnut pan, then she set it on the hearth. To console herself, she said aloud, "When he comes home, we will roast chestnuts."

Nora passed the next few hours on the sofa, her knitting needles clicking furiously. She kept glancing at the clock, which seemed to stand still as long as she watched it. She got up often and looked out the window, hoping to see the truck's lights coming up the farm road. Each time she looked, she could see the snow piling up outside, changing the lines of the land all around the farm. Already one side of the barn was covered in a huge white drift.

She vowed to never again go to sleep without kissing her husband goodnight.

❄

Carl opened his eyes and looked around in a daze. He was in a ditch, the front of the truck pointing at the sky. Through the windshield he saw an angel hovering above him, and as he stared at it, he thought he saw it move. Then he realized he had run into a pillar near the cemetery gate in Lake Florence Township.

"What if that stone angel falls through the windshield?" he thought. And he wondered for just a moment which side of the cemetery

he was on, and what his hope for eternal salvation might be if he were killed by a falling Catholic angel.

"What will people think if they find me here, a Lutheran crushed by a Catholic statue?" thought Carl. He knew the event would have the people back home talking for weeks, his bizarre death a sign of some unknown moral failing.

Carl knew leaving the protection of the truck to look for help could cost him his life. He was trapped and exhausted. He lay his head on the steering wheel and thought about what a dumb idea it had been to race the storm.

As he sat cold and alone, he wished he had stayed home with Nora. Nothing was more important than being with the one you love, especially on Christmas Eve.

It was then he noticed the bag of chestnuts beside him had come open. The small statue of

St. Patrick stared up at him, and even in the darkness, Carl could see the blue eyes shining as though lit by stars. He took the statue from the bag and held it in front of him.

"O'Hara says praying to you won't do any good because I'm Norwegian. I hope he's wrong because I need help," he said, closing his eyes.

"St. Patrick, I don't want to die in this storm, and I don't want to be crushed by a falling angel. I just want to be with my wife. If you can find room in your heart to help a tired Norwegian, then please help me get back home."

Carl opened his eyes and looked up, and a flicker of light in the rearview mirror caught his attention. When he turned around to look, he saw that the light came from a farm just beyond the road. The wind had stopped at last. He knew that if he could somehow get back on the road, he could make it home.

He set the statue beside him and shifted the gears of the truck into reverse. Then he slammed his foot on the gas pedal and grabbed the bag of chestnuts so they wouldn't spill. The tires spun and then caught, and the truck careened up the far side of the ditch. In an instant, Carl was back on the road. He spun the steering wheel but hit a patch of ice and turned more than a full circle before coming to a stop—a stop that, to his amazement, left him pointing the right direction on the county road to go home.

Carl looked back at the cemetery gate and the stone angel. Now the angel seemed harmless, almost as if it were trying to work itself free and fly away. He placed the bag of chestnuts beside him on the seat and eased the truck forward slowly.

Driving home, he looked down at the statue of St. Patrick, and though Carl never quite understood why, he knew he no longer had to be afraid.

❋

It was nearly midnight when Nora thought she heard a horn out on the farm road. She ran to the window and looked out, but all she could see was the reflection of the living room and darkness beyond.

"I'm hearing things," she thought. "I'm going crazy with worry."

She heard it again. This time, she could see two yellow lights glowing faintly in the distance. Nora threw on her coat and ran to the porch. She hurried down the steps as Carl brought the truck to a stop in front of the two small pine trees next to the barn.

Carl's hands slipped from the steering wheel into his lap. He looked down at the statue, now partly hidden under the bag of chestnuts. "Thank you," he whispered.

When Carl stepped out of the truck, Nora ran to him and hugged him so hard that they both fell down in the snow.

"You're home! Thank God, you're home," she said. Carl could see she was crying.

"Easy, sweetheart," he said, flat on his back. "I'm a weak man. I didn't have any breakfast. Only had one egg salad sandwich all day."

"Come inside right now," Nora said with mock sternness. "We'll eat chestnuts."

"How did you know?" he asked.

"Hans Nelson told me that the only reason you'd go to St. Paul was to buy chestnuts."

"It's our first Christmas together, and I wanted to give you what you wished for."

"Carl, you already have. It's our first Christmas as a family. We're beginning our life together. I don't ever want to argue again."

She stood up and helped him to his feet. "Now come in the house and get warm. And promise me you'll never do something like this again, no matter what I wish for," she said.

"Just a minute." He reached into the truck for the bag of chestnuts and the statue of St. Patrick.

"What's that statue?" Nora asked.

"It's a long story," said Carl. "Let me tell you what happened."

He took Nora's hand, and together they went in to warm themselves by the fire.

❊

Carl and Nora Olson called the Christmas of 1931 their Irish Christmas. Just after midnight on Christmas Eve, they placed the statue of St. Patrick on the mantel and held hands while they said a prayer of thanks. Then they roasted chestnuts in the chestnut pan, just as Nora had wished.

On Christmas morning, they were careful to remove the statue before the neighbors stopped by; it would have caused quite a stir if any members of Divine Redeemer had seen it. Carl and Nora also made a promise to each other that Christmas to give their first child an Irish name. The next spring, it caused a bit of a scandal when the baby everyone thought would be named Carl Jr. was instead christened Patrick Sean Olson. He was the only Patrick in all of Franklin Township, and he was my father.

Carl and Nora Olson celebrated many more Christmases together in Franklin Township. As time passed, their family grew, and each Christmas, the Olson children and grandchildren, and then great-grandchildren, would gather around the fire at the farm-house to roast chestnuts in Nora Olson's chestnut pan.

*J*ON LOOKED AT HIS DAUGHTER, who was now sitting in Nora's rocking chair. "So that's the story of the chestnut pan," he said.

"I love that story, Daddy," Kari replied. "How long will our tradition last?"

"As long as there is Christmas and chestnuts and the Olsons," he answered, but in his heart he wondered.

"And don't forget St. Patrick," said Kari.

"And St. Patrick," said Jon with a smile. "Now, Kari, go get the potholder so I can pull the pan out of the fire. And tell everyone to come in and gather 'round. It's time to eat the chestnuts."

She looked at him with a puzzled expression. "But, Daddy, everyone's already here," she said, amazed that he hadn't noticed.

Jon looked over his shoulder to see the rest of the family quietly settled on the sofa and the edge of the rug.

"Don't burn the chestnuts, or we won't let you roast them next year," said his wife with a chuckle.

As he heard the familiar words, Jon realized that whether they kept the farm or not wasn't important. They were family. Wherever life took the Olsons, they would find a way to roast chestnuts together every Christmas Eve. And the story of how their tradition began would be passed down by Kari to her children, and from her children to theirs. Nora Olson's death did not mean this Christmas was the end of the story—it was, just as Nora always said, "a time of new beginnings."

Carl and Nora's Recipe for Roasting Chestnuts over an Open Fire

Carefully cut an "X" into the rounded side of the shell with a sharp knife. Place the chestnuts flat side down in a single layer in the chestnut pan. Gently shake the pan over the fire until the nuts "open," about 10–15 minutes. Serve warm.

If you want to roast other nuts in the shell, try peanuts, pecans, walnuts, Brazil nuts, pistachios, or cashews.

Remember, the chestnut pan will be very hot, so use an oven mitt.

And . . .

"Don't burn the chestnuts,
or we won't let you roast them next year!"

A portion of the proceeds of this book will go to Fr. Tom Hagan, O.S.F.S. and the miracle workers of *Hands Together* who provide education, medical care, food, and love to the poor in Haiti.

Acknowledgments

The author would like to thank:

Jeannie C. Barnum

Lynne Bertalmio

Robert Breck

Kathy Buckstaff

Bill Ersland

The Gang at Writers Unlimited

Fr. Tom Hagan, O.S.F.S.

Vicki Harris

Helen Horton

The Horton Family Children

Dan Kiernan

Mary Kiernan

Deb Lysholm

Mary Miller

The People of Dent, Minnesota

Sue Primeau

Boni Roberts

Janean Stadler

Jessica Thoreson

Dan Verdick

Elizabeth Verdick

Jill Wade

Jim Wallace

Beth Wegner